MIDWATCH

Midwatch

Graves Registry, Parts IV and V

Keith Wilson

The Sumac Press
Fremont, Michigan

—Illustrations by Lucy Evans

LIBRARY OF CONGRESS CATALOGUE CARD NUMBER 73-181816
STANDARD BOOK NUMBERS:
Paper edition 912090-14-6
Cloth edition 912090-15-4

Cafe Solo, Changes Frontiers (New Zealand), *Human Voice,
Hiram Poetry Review, ARX, Monk's Pond, Weed / Flower, Dragonfly,
Pebble, Wasatch Front*

The poems "STARCHART" and "STARSONG" appear in
INSIDE OUTER SPACE, copyright 1970 by Doubleday & Company.

—for Heloise

. . . Wer kanns unterscheiden?
Rilke

Table of Contents

GRAVES REGISTRY, PART IV   SEA CHANTEYS

Ballad of a Sailor   11
Seacaptain   14
Graves Registry IV: The Poem Politic   15
MidWatch   17
The Poem Politic ii   19
Seadream   20
How to Sit Here at this Desk Smiling?   22
Seastories   24
The Poem Politic iii   26
The Rotting Hawser   27
Seachanty: Burial Song   28
The Poem Politic iv   31
The Seacaptain Speaks of Prophecy   33
StarSong   34
SeaPiece   36
The Poem Politic v   37
Seachanty: Night Song   39
The Poem Politic vi   42
The SeaCaptain, To a Junior Officer   43
The Poem Politic vii   44
Seachanty: Driftwood   46
The Poem Politic viii   50
StarChart   51
The Poem Politic ix   52
The SeaCaptain's Song   54
The Poem Politic x: A Note for Future Historians   55

GRAVES REGISTRY, PART V   COMMENTARY

The Ring of Annapolis: Sea as it touches land   61
graves registry, part v   65
Navigational Fix   66
Sad Child   68
Memory of a Victory   69
iii Peace   70
iv   71
Drift Wood   72
v   73
vi   74
The Drowned Boy   75
vii The Dream   76
Corsair   77
viii   81
A Love Song for some Later Time: My Skeleton Hand   82
ix   83
x   84
the callings   85

Preface

the badges

We make them, to reassure ourselves.
We pretend.
Walk by with plumed helmets.
Wear noble orders, get prizes.
Nod to shadowy crowds.
All of us
Heroes.   Kings.

Graves Registry, Part IV
SeaChanteys

Ballad of a Sailor

> *. . . wave,*
> *interminably flowing*
> —Wallace Stevens

It is because my fingers
move over these keys
compulsively
that the result
> *quiets me*

Dark images of war,
storms, hands raised like waves
in my dreams the wind
never stops

betrayed shores
sick girls in foreign bars
children begging outside
a night that is always closed

Comrades, their drowning faces
pale tourmaline, rayed with light,
open eyes and seawashed mouths

It is because my fingers
move over these keys
restlessly
that the chanty
> *moves me*

11

Here, far from the sea,
this house is steady.   It does
not rock and that noise is
thunder, not gunfire.   It is
peaceful here.   Say it again.
Peaceful.   One has only to stay
awake, not dream, the faces of dreams
cannot touch, dreamed blood stains
only the bedsheet sails of haunted ships.

Sailing, sail on, its crew of phantoms
wave, passing beyond the light, wave
& giggle among the shrouds, knowing
it is not the last goodbye nor the first
we are sharing.

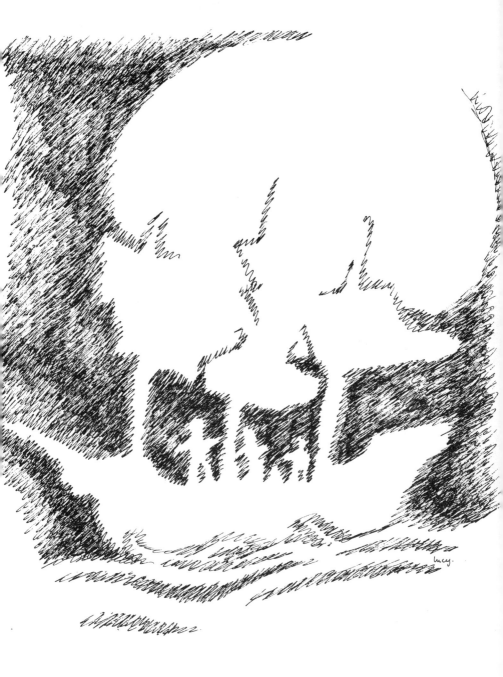

Seacaptain

I never belonged to you.

Always the wind blew clean
& fresh to my face.

My friends are deadvoices.
My loves, the seas breaking
upon discarded conchshells.

I never belonged
but heard always

deadmouths crying through the fog
touched coolsteel at night, salt
winds rising, and far away
the buck & heave of a nunbuoy's bell.

I never.   I'm sorry.
I listened always.
The seacrystals of my breath
& the rigging stiffbearded with ice,
seawinds that no longer call a specific name.

The world, hulled down, glistens
disappears with the horizon, night
closing behind the darkening wake.

Graves Registry IV: The Poem Politic

i

an afterword

Statements.   The words
collecting themselves, make
chattering sounds.   The TV fills
with words.

He is dead.
John Fitzgerald Kennedy.
Martin Luther King.
Medgar Evers.
Jesus of Nazareth.
Malcolm X.
Peter, Called Simon.
Alexander II of Serbia.
Robert Francis Kennedy.

The TV fills livingrooms
with the wordcaskets of dead men.
Flashes faces, killers and killed.
Emerson said, "The Brahma."
What is killed, is hard to see.
Residue: bodies, blood, pictures.

Electrons bouncing off a sensitized
screen, form to our eyes, visions:
RFK lies on the floor bleeding slightly.
Later, a dark young man coolly
looks back.

In Viet Nam, soldiers cut testicles
from five other men. They too
lie and bleed.   Soon they will
die, as their generations died in
the act of the knife

Our President sadly declaims
men-of-violence, not seeing the blood
seeping under the White House doors.

MidWatch

—Captain, from his quarterdeck

I would only wish you
happiness

    & yet I rage
& lunge against the night, cry
a name not yours, speak the terrible
words She gave me, put upon my lips
this strange song

Here, with the darkness like chains
about me, I dream of you, would touch
your breast, put my head beside yours—

Know that.   I give courses for others,
lay out tracks on snowy, fresh charts
& all the while I am in the grip
of a current that sweeps me along
through the gutting rock & the seabird's
harsh cries

    From wherever I am I only wish you
love & take another turn about the deck
of this cramped room, this turning street.
We are not always what we say we are.
I, not always what I would be, for you.

Yet, here, caught now in this midnight
madness, seeing with more clarity than
this lamp should allow, I know I follow
another, Her thin hair caught to an
Easterning breeze, sudden gusts to catch
Her silver hair & lash it out like snakes
while the wood groans & cries in Her
voice about me.   Seahag, figurehead of the
dark nightwatches the new moon catches
Her bony back & I must follow in the hollowed
shadows of Her eyes, the wrecking coasts,
the torn skies flapping like sail
canvas, the ruinous cries of birds
& broken bells . . . .

I would wish you somewhere else
than here, some other love than mine.
And take my turn beside the wheel.

The Poem Politic ii

No body dies, the spirit lives
its long agonies through eternities of dreams:
one life gouged out of a body, is one life,
calls from whatever distant crags of light
for others.   The dead always needing companions.

We cannot stop violence with violence.   We cannot
stop violence at all, feeding as we do on
the bloody carcasses of our brothers,
our friend-animals.   There is nothing and
no body we will not eat.   Kill to feed
our children and send our children
to their deaths, speaking fine wordtombs
to hold each shattered body: Here lies
Timmy, who made his dear old father proud.
The endless heaps of photographs, learning
to walk, in his Boy Scout uniform, graduating
for field green.   His first stripes.   The last
sitting on a sealed casket containing, one hopes,
Timmy.

no body dies.   the flesh rots, turns blue
then black.   a time of fierce activity.   chemically.
electrically.   never more alive, than at death.

The young girl, disemboweled by a stray
artillery round, is not dead.   One has only
to look at her writhing on the damp earth
to see her vitality

19

Seadream

Before this light
what eyes, but mine,
were caught to this color?

dark waves, foam
colored to froth
bones, bones
to ride darkgreen crests

      —ghosts, thin
faces
    a wave here
there, a destiny sails
beyond a horizon always
beyond
    a color, changing
    to a new light

2

Old men
who stand
beside the sea
. . . fading eyes,
leaning on canes
crippled gulls
fighting the blue
crying, they disappear

3

bright, bright sails!

Endlessly sailing ships
setting forever courses, taff-rail
logs cutting their thin wakes

a sun, going
copper, brightly
lighted the figure head,
a young firm girl
with a seashattered
face

golden gulls, crying
"Death!" as they swoop
Eastward the night
opens its black rose

How To Sit Here At This
Desk Smiling?

How long can I continue to act
a part of this country?

                This country.
This beloved land, its slashing
storms and great upthrust mountains,
meadows green and brown, bright under
the clear, sharp sun.

This country where my red brothers
were slaughtered—their gods call
their names from every hill—
where my black brothers, enslaved,
dying scream their pain from cities
darkened and grey with the ruin
of mountains

                & any protest against
a destruction, so clearly seen, gets met
with bayonets, with mace, with clubs
rising and falling, blooded to their tips

How to sit here at this desk, smiling,
nodding my head when my fists are clenched
on its polished wood and I give, by my
presence, credence to. Their crushing
smashing hatred of this land, of all
that is growing or green

                young or beautiful?

Flowers germinate, raise their blunt
stalks to find concrete sealing them
from the sun; babies cough out their
lives and we wash & wash & wash & wash

How to sit here at this desk smiling?

Seastories

A form of lies
of course, stories,
tales told while
the wind, the small
lights of water
catch the eye,
lie

—in ancient triemes,
oars, as Homer spoke it,
filled the singing air
with gull wings, crisp
white wood held in lighted
centuries, pineknot torches
reflecting against patched sails

—my old Mate, himself
a drinker, yet holding
in scarred hands a knowing
past the sense of his sagging
eyes

(a crazy seaman born without
fear, if you can imagine that!
sticking his curly grey head
out a hawser hole while the chain
roared hugely by, grinning
as the anchor hook plunged
to an unknown bottom)

—the fierce rise of wind
to signal a storm caught
flapping in colored flags
warning, briefly, of the many days
you'll spend fighting, begging giant waves
not to destroy the thin shell
carrying you, whoever you are

How quietly this shorefire flickers.
The Benedictine follows the dinner
round and round this tiny glass.
Her eyes watch you & for a moment
you feel almost like explaining
what it is to shout out your longing
to a storm, or to love in a way
you could never love her
—the salt you washed off your skin.

The Poem Politic iii

"What are politics anyway
but the formalized lusts and greeds of men?

Dancing figures around a straining body,
the knife is raised high, glints in candle
light the blood is purple, stuff of Kings,
with one high scream the manthing dies
for religion or fun or policy or nothing
at all that any reasonable man can explain."

So spoke the philosopher, carefully
poisoning his home with flyspray.

The Rotting Hawser

Brightness.   And we must
die.   Darkening seawinds,
salt caught fresh on the eyelids,
young muscles under clean shirts
cleaner sails catching full

            —a tricky wake, but we
too slip away, full moon or no
moon at all, heavy with our loves,
our whiskied dreams, shouted loneliness
as we pass

            strand by strand, the
cables slip and with a snap! the little
craft we have

            the sea claiming her loan
jiggers of Island rum caught in a brown light
a clink, and the thrown glasses disappear,
winding their trails of bubbles, sinking,
move down, a few sharp glints to mark
a slender, laughing trail . . . .

Seachanty: Burial Song

*blow the man down, laddies, blow
the man
down . . .*

And speak over his bier the songs
spent in ancient time hauling
a capstan winch or shouted
drunk to the bars of the world.

Let friendship be a passing
sealight, which promised safety
while we sailed on to the next port.

Burn his candles low, since we
are paying for them and instead
of dust, cast salt, seasalt
—that's important.   Let every man
know that here's a sailor and we
loved him.   He should be buried
at sea, there's the thing, don't
you know?   But he died ashore.
So sprinkle a little salt on him
that he'll know he's home once more.

Chorus

the wind howls past
the saltspun bar, the reef
with its screaming seabirds

and strange is the port
we come to, the girls
with dried lips and gusty
eyes to meet us, sailors,
come from the seas

so let no man blow you down,
laddie, let no man get your windward . . .

I speak to you not of oceans
but of the desperate time I've had
making you understand.

It's a strange world
and whether you sail
upon the seas or walk
hatless and supperless
on the land, the great waves
of sky break above you.

You have heard the sea
bird's cried dream.   The taste
of longing before your eyes
grew dark watching the circling
fish, the green, green water
bubbles following you down
to the sand where you kissed
and the grains stuck to your lips.

no man blew you down, laddie.
it was the nature of the papers you signed,
the cargo of your voyage.

The Poem Politic iv

We must open ourselves here in America.
We must strain our eyes to see
the colors of a land we are filling
with hatreds.   A man who will casually
kill a tree, will as easily kill his
own kind.   The tree is as important
as any brigade, any old man looking
out from under his white eyebrows.

> "We executed an old man like that
> in Korea.   A village elder, he never
> knew why, I don't think.   We shot him
> at the base of the skull, though he
> refused to take his funny hat off.
> There was almost no blood until we
> rolled him over.   Then we saw the
> front of his face was gone.   The
> bullet shouldn't have done that.
> Ballistically, it should have continued
> its downward path, but it probably hit
> the backbone, was deflected up.   It can
> be explained, of course.   But I don't know
> why we did it either."
>
> Major J.E.K., U.S.A.

The horrors that fill us, atrocities
under another man's hand, cram our own
dreams and memories

A bomb I loaded on a plane was dropped
by a killcrazy kid pilot on a courtyard
full of refugees.   He spoke excitedly
of bodies, arms, legs that rose several
hundred feet in the air.   The walls of
the courtyard contained the explosion,
forcing it upward, a fountain of flesh.

Though I, personally, did not touch
the button—my own handiwork.

The Seacaptain Speaks of Prophecy

In the name of Atlantis, Thule, & Mu,
seacoffins rising!

       Ships snake their courses,
guywires humming like guitars, while
new Americas break through the waves
to crossed lanterns; flashing in children
canyons of seas open up.   The stars become
singers no pause for thought the age has
flashed a nightmare across the sky and
leaves, in an idiot's hand, a royal token.

StarSong

Old voyages to be had:
—stars flaming in the lensed glasses
    sextants cold to the hand's touch
    certain glimpses of a blackness
    beyond stars

Comets burn into a Way
slash past galaxies

theories, worded & symbolled gropings
never suffice to capture the shadow,

its center pulsing, an energy
flaming in the hearts of mountains

Shadows, young feet in sandals
bright thighs held in silk banners,
sex-mounted, two-backed beasts
their rhythms pounding out through
time: background
                        of the dying, their breaths
hollow in the chest's escapement

            all part of the vision
            the moment passes, comet
            it leaves a trail marked
            in the green surfaces
            of your eyes

                    startled
the world draws back, slips
through planes slicing sliding
in motion, harmonies appear
momentary

                  as love is not.

I love you
now, touch you in my sleep
I reach, make love you never
waken I forget the bright blaze
light forever before our eyes
we sleep, wince away, the darkness
under our lids disturbed, all energies
held together in the moistness, body
upon body—strange journeys!

Visions, changing shadows to guard
us, our transcendent lunges, the light
surrounding us pries open our eyes &
look! we are not blind in the heat of this fire
we see, we see! through landscapes of worlds
dying, spinning out tired histories new blood
young dreams, echoes from the stars, children
to the loin's mysteries.

SeaPiece

Deep ruby lights, held
hard by the darkening water:
grey slips of fishes, tugboats
heading—serious old women!
hooting out the buoyed lanes

       —seadrifts, small precise
callings, clumped like drowned children,
hair shining with plankton, eyes
of death's own stars
          ****

Ripples, gentle surface movements
where huge fish heavily stir
giant tails, deep, where the masts
of broken ships lie beside

                    ruby eyes.
The sea, constrained by its own weight
where it is; the rush of blood above flows
through the channeled sailor's body

       —somewhere, a ship lies off
a dark coast, carrying who knows what
terrible cargo?

Deep, deep eyes of the sea
endless cold stirrings of the bottom's
salty winds

The Poem Politic v

Within the prisons of our lives,
the dark necessities of breathing, eating
defecating—the nearly constant pain of
some ache or bone awareness, blinding
toothaches, gut growlings, cuts bruises
and contusions
                    within the white cages
of our bones, the red veils of blood
in tiny webbings, caught as we are
in the centered lattices of nerves, fluids,
stiffened bones

                    Lies what?   A vision?
A kind of awareness that can see
canyons, gulfs blue and stretching
inside so wide that clouds form
oceans roar

    a voice, speaking & shouting
roars, roars, roars . . . .

Are we separate from the ocean?   Does
the tree shade us, or make us?   Above
everything, the ghostsun dies endlessly
yet follows its molten death.

    I have seen that.
    I can bear witness to that.

(no body dies.
we must not kill.
eat, or you will die.)

Don't try to trick me
by leaving off the questionmarks.
Those are questions, all right,
and I don't want to hear them.

Let me alone, I have funerals to attend.
In this great graveyard, this huge spinning
tomb, the work of burial goes on.   That is the
final politic, death wins all the polls, holds
all offices, claims the war and the warrior . . . .

Seachanty: Night Song

—SeaCaptain, on the bridge

To get this all spoken
OUT

The twisted mocking echoes
that shadow my thoughts, let
them fall, softly, snowflakes
on deserted windows, words with
gleaming copper edges—steam
from a teapot & a kitchen

—that little girl in Portugal
who in her silence her torment
her acceptance of her role, offered
hands that began at the elbow,
fingers curling out like confetti

      the soft young face
of destiny, her clear eyes & pig
tails begging for an *escudo*

Not to be forgotten, this park
where I waited for a girl &
found a child

Memories, curling back
woodchips from my greatuncle's
sharp knife, cutting dreams from
a knurl of wood, a whittled sixgun to hold
gleaming oak bulletends & protect
the child from the night, or the darkness
from the child that stalks within us all.

ii

Some one said that this night, these
snubbed candles shall be the last.   A
victory in anything that is the last.

Meanwhile we wait, hoping that tomorrow's
dawn, while coming, will not be seen by us.

A satisfaction in finality.   An end to some
thing.   The whole group of us, testing this moment,
knowing it is all a lie.   It never stops, we go
on, on, on

Above some hill, the moon rises.
Soon will come the sun, and the sea
will glow emerald, the breeze will be sweet.

iii

I would ask you of where you've travelled
since last we met.

Was it Singapore or Chitzen Itza,
Maracaibo or the Straights of Ur?
Memphis or the deep channels of Mindanao?

On frail ships, on our feet bare to coral
sand and snakes we venture forth, knowing
not which dawn will bring which revelation:

We go to sea, or life, like insects
riding a board, full of brave songs
frightened of puddles or the reflections
of our own faces . . . . .

iv

To get it all spit out—the tireless reminders,
whispered voices of past lovers, cracked skin
shaved in the mirrors of hundreds of yesterdays.

Small girl of Lisbon, naked dancer of Paris,
the flowers of Cuban streets, baritone who sang
too well for the bar he was in, the face of a pilot
dying as his jet sank in the Yellow Sea, fighting
the canopy—beautiful word!—yet he was dead.

A chanty, then, born of rum & wine, girls who might
remember you when they are old and their lovely
breasts have shrunk to sacks, deeplined & dry . . .

Eyes that hold in themselves the diamond lights
of a sky we think we see; out of so much pain,
an exorcism for the living which alone seems
beautiful, or worthy, riding our bobbing boards.

The Poem Politic vi

I don't know what government means.
Who can understand men.   A man or two,
here and there—I can cope with that,
come even to love them, place my arms
about them, and cry at their deaths.

Leave me alone with your government.
I have too many to mourn now.

The SeaCaptain, To a Junior Officer

Listen, these times beat about us
—wardrums *we* have heard before!   We
do not panic, holding fast the courses
we have set, we wait the time when our pennants,
flaring with the SunOrb, royal diadem of mastery,
take the seas again as our own

                           Do not despair.
Life ebbs and flows, we count the years with knots
on a shiplog's line, held out to currents of blue,
bright streams that mark a wake too long for calendars.

We go to sea, yes; but always our feet are aware
of the earth lying beneath the water, palaces
where we lived, tombs that bear our ancient names.

The Poem Politic vii

These as days, pass, keep
their pace, nodding, let us
sleep who would never awake

soldiers!   We are all soldiers
(in the sense that we are victim
to wars: our lives themselves, killer

        —moving onward the Christian
banner ahead, gutted children behind
smoke, gas bayonet landmines

beyond one horizon, or another,
the quick sails of warships
gunmuzzles glinting in moonlight

shadows across graves
broken lances, arrows
the shock of cannon
still haunting valleys

Where in America
can you go
that a battle has not been fought
men killed?

in the night
lynched men hang in their trees

leaves ripple
with summer winds

the past, so rapidly
becoming the future,
old graves to welcome
the wanderer

Where in America
can you go?

Seachanty: Driftwood

—the SeaCaptain to his dead love,
walking beside her

a fragility of lips.

stones, dropping through
into blue blue depths.

the color of a girl's eyes
as she is dying, the blood
we leave behind is shadow

falling as moons, bones
and stones, the echoes of us,
what we are or were—not end
less

but continuing, held
to a lantern's glare our faces
tear like tissue, eyes stare out
beyond longing

or belonging

—steel flakes in oil or gold
caught on the hand, briefly
glistening, sand from a beach

we are what we hold longest
to or from

ii

these feet pressing sands
that once were mine in days
of sand-dollar stars, crisp
seawinds to catch up a girl's
hair and spread it like a net

to seine those same stars with

I have no memory.
Only the traced days lining
this temporary face.   Do not
expect me to remember and instead
hold me hold me

iii

his love, replying

oh come here touch me
do not remain forever barren
beating your fists against
the cliffs of your own mind

I am a wind and I blow
through you.   I am a sea

all of me, deep with your
flesh, raging with your eyes

we two, we are a storm
come upon a shore, a raven
cawing for its dead, a terrible
smile on the face of the moon.

if I am a wind you are the tree
I bend but never break, as a sea
I shape the shore, a light
beyond the breakers is your cry

          I, I never die
but grope against dreaming tides
move in, move out, in motion, born
whirling, shouting out my name,
names, as the grained sands of universes
echo to another, the seahigh scream
of what cannot be spoken

The Poem Politic viii

We have had enough of history!
—the telling of old tales, blood
haunted with nights of children
breaking anew to the horror and
false glory of dying for causes
or simply because

         Can a child
be taught *not* to kill, when he crushes
the baby chicken so easily under his heel,
fingers his wooden sword and howls
with apechild anger?

            Our loves
wear tattered gowns, our hatreds
shining steel and battleflags

We, as men, walk aimlessly
through the fields of horror
mumbling of our God, fearing
our own inner nights, the space
we know opens for us, contains
us not

      *Children, creatures
of the night, light winds
hold your hair against a moon
that knew your fathers
crazed your mothers*

*Children, how do you walk
tonight, your little knives
glistening in the hollow light?*

50

StarChart

Bending my already stiff fingers
to the words & signs I can catch,
following to the limits of my ability
that which I, and I alone, can seize
hold

        —still I know some starship
will arrive, burst casually forth
with poems

        Crystals held in the hand!
        Activated by one's own energy!
        Triggering brainresponses
        without words!　A high singing
        of the bones!

Poems greater than those I hear
but cannot yet, even granted the limits
of a medium heavy with printed pages
speak

We are only men
gesturing in the fog & smoke
of time past & time to come

We,
sailing from one charted dot
to another, the whole planet
hurtling through unmapped space.

The Poem Politic ix

Let us make a new Compact,
this time with the land.

Let us hold it, try to
understand how to live
with it, not just on it

. . . Holding cupped hands
about the fire we bring
it, let us be warm
move our houses
root them like trees
so that they blend
not shout, look, look
at ME

    god damn it,
let's forget about ME,
and worry about who
this I-sore thing is
we carry about through
our dusty years

    my friend says
if you want to preach
go down South they
need you there

               O.K.   How far
South?
                    Past the rotting
rivers, dying trees, the gutted
clays and rocks and sticks and mud
pissed and rooted up and poisoned

What spots have we missed?

Forget it.   The land wants
no part of us.   It looks
with Indian eyes (the old
gods still there, beyond the hills
and the rivers, their curse
upon us, our murders

darken every flower)

The SeaCaptain's Song

Far, far lie the silences—
following the sun, borne triumphant,
the air carries a title, an emblem
expanding towards glory . . . .

Recent touches, hands, lips,
the swift impotence of years
too long, too spent in the opening
—Petals that shatter the sun!—

> *the swift, small moments*
> *that lie in your hands*

Lost, as these my own fingers
are lost in the ageroughened
reality of what I feel in you, denying
nothing, and therefore open to all.

My palms are plains upon which
a record of battle is spread:
a dark night of the Mounts,
swelling, changing.

These scars are deeply engrained.
Under them are bones, and under
the bones . . . stars, hurtling atoms,
a universe of forces, pre-existent,
reaching like a doom for your face.

The Poem Politic x: A Note for Future Historians

When writing of us, state
as your first premise
THEY VALUED WAR MORE THAN ANYTHING
You will never understand us
otherwise, say that we

cherished war

    over peace and comfort
    over feeding the poor
    over our own health
    over love, even the act of it
    over religion, all of them, except
    perhaps certain forms of Buddhism

that we never failed to pass bills of war
through our legislatures, using the pressures
of imminent invasion or disaster (potential)
abroad as absolution for not spending moneys
on projects which might make us happy or even
save us from clear and evident crises at home

Write of us that we spent millions educating
the best of our youth and then slaughtered them
capturing some hill or swamp of no value and
bragged for several months about how well they died
following orders that were admittedly stupid, ill-conceived

Explain how the military virtues, best practiced
by robots, are most valued by us.   You will never come
to understand us unless you realize, from the first,
that we love killing and kill our own youth, our own great
men FIRST.   Enemies can be forgiven, their broken bodies
mourned over, but our own are rarely spoken of except in
political speeches when we "honor" the dead and encourage
the living young to follow their example and be gloriously
dead also

NOTE: Almost all religious training, in all our countries,
dedicates itself to preparing the people for war.
Catholic chaplains rage against "peaceniks," forgetting
Christ's title in the Church is Prince of Peace;
Baptists shout of the ungodly and the necessity of
ritual holy wars while preaching of the Ten
                              Commandments
each Sunday; Mohammedans, Shintoists look forward
to days of bloody retribution while Jews march
across the sands of Palestine deserts, Rabbis
urging them on . . . .

THEY VALUE WAR MORE THAN ANYTHING

Will expose our children, our homes to murder and
devastation on the chance that we can murder or devastate
FIRST and thus gain honor.   No scientist is respected
                                                    whose
inventions help mankind, for its own sake, but only when
those discoveries help to destroy, or to heal people,
that they may help destroy other men and living things

56

                                    Be aware that
Destiny has caught us up, our choices made
subtly over the ages have spun a web about us:
It is unlikely we will escape, having geared
everything in our societies toward war and combat.
It is probably too late for us to survive
in anything like our present form.

THEY VALUED WAR MORE THAN ANYTHING

If you build us monuments let them all
say that, as warning, as a poison label
on a bottle, that you may not ever
repeat our follies, feel our griefs.

Graves Registry, Part V
Commentary

The Ring of Annapolis: Sea, as it touches land

the tide.

1

what comes in, the drift
out, drift beyond
        gulls hang
        in the seamists
        the sun
is rich in oranges, the
whole spectrum, purples, reds
greens, low lights of oil
        halfobscured by standing
        mist: a stationary
        world, ship
        a dot at
        center
        —fruitmarkets of the sea
        glorious with surprise!

2

(anthony, new mexico)

these present dark
green fields, cotton
blooms in yellow
& red, in pale
hills the wind
clouds, sweeps
the valley clean
of stars

at my elbow Hell
is a falling star
a closing world

the shore.

3

cool green.   lost
eyes drowned in jade.
old friends.
pulling out my heart.

—a huge stone, my ring, it
is the sea, the whole
sea, one jewel reflecting
light, going out . . .

4

&
what the passions come
to, beyond which bounds
they break free: in
raw color image shines
beckons

      —Blake's God.
      the spread fingers are
      twin lightnings

          :passion, memory
flare, discharging the sensed
thing lost, finitely
dear, driving, driving me
on

         from these fields from
that sea, the green the blue ascend
the brain to snap to spark
to reach out past rock past mountain,
field, the spilling sea

        —until all stands in memory:

the predictable equation,
man + senses + age = recall,
a flooding of passion through
the remembered

                    and lost birds are set
          flying

          the predictable equation
          transmuted to flesh
          snares universes, holds them
          singing in the hand

graves registry, part v

the wars go on & on
stretching out backwards

forwards like bands marching
men steel old shouts lavender

air.   they say I am a war poet.
what's a war poet?   I often

ask myself this question, knowing
the cannonfire my brain was born to

the battlefields marked heavily
on my aging skin, dream toward roman

victories, celtic princes, battleaxes
and missiles, the flow of the blood

is touched with bayonets, the flash
of gunfire is in the yes eyes and no

where is there peace, stretching out
backwards forwards the bands marching

Navigational Fix

a plot
taken

starlines
intersect, tell

a steel ship
where it

is: under
flaming distant

suns safety
hides in crossed

pencil
lines

a dot
just *there*

waves towering
around it
.

I am an older man now.
The battles of my youth

as the present explodes
about me, the sad flares

crimsoned eyes and echoed
laughs that ring today

make yesterday seem . . .
someone else's movie, tales

from a younger brother's horrors
told, with embarrassment

over an unaccustomed drink,
his uniform still stiff and new.

That boy was me, I, that boy
his hand slips too easily

into my skin, his glove,
he moves the fingers to touch

my eyes are an old man's eyes
my heart knows too many wars

too many lost roads that turn
beyond this last light, this day

he walks along whistling, dark
with me, calling, calling uneasily.

Sad Child

Speaking of the wind's remembrances,
calling with small eyes out to the sky.
Beside the road.   One hand up.
The other behind his back
the whole troop of shadows
mocking whispers that cry out
an eternity against his moment
shroud blue eyes with grey reaching hands

Memory of a Victory

Off the Korean Coast, beyond Wonsan
waiting for invasion soft winds blew
the scent of squid drying in the sun,
homely smells of rice paddies, cooking fires.

It was a picture world with low hills
much like New Mexico, except for water,
the strange smells.   Little plumes of smoke.
Here & there, the glint of steel.

Under the waiting guns lay peachblossoms.
I could see them with my binoculars.
The planes still had not come, all eternity
waited beneath the sweep second hand.

Then the crackling radio commanded
"Fire!" and a distant world I could have loved
went up in shattering bursts, in greyblack explosions,
the strange trees that suddenly grew on the hillside.

They fired their rifles, light howitzers
back.   After awhile we sent boats into the silence.

iii
Peace

War rises swiftly
in the blood, arrowheads
Roman spears the slash
of bladed hours

What kind of fierce comment
is this, to leave behind, to give up
that which makes a man
feel *most* alive?   most wanted

by his women?

Females have no respect for men
who will not fight unless their pacifism
is also a way of fighting, war in the eyes.

iv

What shall we leave for the children?
What lying myths of grandfathers
who killed Indians, trafficked in slaves,
held life, even their own, cheaply
without worth, beyond the dying well?

Holes, children, holes we leave you
hoping you will fill them.   Hollowed
circles of night, earthdaughters to love you,
peaceful warriors of sunlight to walk beside you.
The deep scars of our living, enough for you.

DriftWood

Little pieces, he picks from the sea.
Assembles them, heavy with the water,
the starstruck wood glistens in the sun
& when thrown, as far as a boy's arm may reach
sinks with soft bubbles . . . . .

V

I've lived enough years now.   Still
they stretch onward: we all come
slowly at first, to this turning.

He is back from the new war.
At Sumer, it was much the same
—Father displaying the son's new
shield, hanging it beside his own,
proud of the swordmarks on both

or mourned privately, and alone,
the absent boy

                    Fierce apes

creatures of a twisted sun, corrupt
hours spent denying a kinship
with other blooded animals, pride only
in glories of conquest, the land soaked
with our urine and hurled into the faces
of yet living enemies of our own kind.

I love you is a whisper spoken
between battles and to a woman of our own race.

vi

Ghosts walk, here in the memory.
I have lived a thousand lives or more,
so have you, and you, and you, but our brains
are recent ones, we live in the ruins of castles
and forget we built them:

      sad birds flying
      about the battlements,
      our old loves, banners
      to a fresh breeze

Richard Coeur de Leon, Hannibal, Gilgamesh-
Enkidu lunging through our nights, claiming
their lists of victories in troubled sleep.
We live upon but one star, among many.

74

The Drowned Boy

The small boy
too long born from within
breaks like a sad, heavy wave.

From the shore, caught to time,
nothing.   A log against the horizon?
Someone's love, a nothing.   Drifting.

The Dream

Stars.　Planets whirling our souls
to a viable aware rhythm, poems
that take the place of battlecries
in a better, coming world of peace.

I tried to tell a womanpoet about this—
the desperate need of shamen, how they shape
the dying eyes of men, grow boys toward
another world, leaving daggers behind.

Some will take words as meaningless,
of little importance beyond the power
they tentatively grant.　No, it is not so.
Words hold the residue of harms, must be taken
thusly, carefully, the flame licking inside them
never goes out, we lift them like rubies
& catch the new sun to freshen their lights.

She plays with Hell
who does not observe the duty
of WordMakers.

Corsair

—to D.S.

It was of course Don
who died.

   —Blue, with white letters
     inverted gull
     P & W engine

At full roar, one by
one they returned.

Minus him.

It was of course of course
my friend

       in the twisted aluminum
       the shining spars
       crumpled wheels

       rudder torn off
       white letter "V"

       splattered with
       ricepaddy mud

It was of course he
who refused, who would not
kill, would not obey, would
not return—refused

77

to machinegun civilians
on the Korean hillside

to bomb a courtyard
full of refugees

It was I on the bridge
of the carrier, waiting
counting the planes—marked
the return of the squadron leader,
he who taught him that

>low, slow turn
>just above stalling speed
>the fighter's controls mush
>there, aces away from a spin

He spun.   He lay
there and I of course
wait, wait for whatever
second coming there can be
for a splattered flyer
my friend, lying there

who would not kill idly
who did not have the dangerous look
who should've should've fired

—Arjuna, it is not your friends
   you kill but only the shadows
   hiding their selves, Arjuna
   whose spear also rusted in the sun

   jagged metal
   the blue, Navy

blue and a crashed corsair fighter
over 20 years old and most probably
no longer there

               a white "V"

to mark another strange victory

viii

WarriorPriests.   Aztec, Commanche, Sioux
Men who past the time of boys singing
in ceremonial chambers live out the slender
sorrows of their manhood, grow to this light
this fierce demand:

                    to lead warriors
away from war, but without peaceful lies.
To show them the challenges of the bones,
brief flickering of these lives that pass
and come, move onward in funeral splendor.

                    My grandfather is me
                    we look out of the same
                    portrait, wear skin
                    and jewels and fur
                    drink from deep glasses

It was the purpose of these poems to show
the glories of war, sadnesses of peace.

Replace them both.

A Love Song for some Later Time:
My Skeleton Hand

men's hands
are joined bones
trembling in the light

I touch you, so

on your skin
I leave a brief mark
palewhite fingerprint
against the pink smoothness

a long time ago
I saw my skeleton hand in a dream
and the bones were whiter
than that mark

what if I were
to touch you to your
cheekbone with my
rough fingertip

and our skulls
rolled together
in a dusty wind

would you hear my teeth
whistle "love"
and know it
was me?

ix

Being more Indian than White, my soul
walks the Yellow Path, fighting with songs
the gentle darkness of Night's Daughter, loving
her more than most . . . .

> Chants beside the River,
> prayerfeathers and *pahos*
> catching desert winds
> celebrating scorpions
> the thrust of cactus

Everything that lives is my equal.
I may *not* kill that I may eat
without permission of the killed.   This
and only this is the Lesson.
Death and Life are the same.

Somewhere in Washington, in Rome,
the War Office in Bucharest, in Sofia,
Moscow

      —in the great cities of Europe
and America, there is The Book.
I have always imagined it black
calves leather with heavy gold letters:

GRAVES REGISTRY

(By now of course each book is fat
swollen with its names and places.
Gigantic, the one in Washington
would bulge the largest room, still
growing hourly with the dead and lost
of the country.   Their names, insofar
as each could be identified.   Next
of Kin, if any.   The nature of the death,
when known.)

Murdered civilians and the enemy
are not there.   Only those who died
in battle or later, in their beds,
their brains burning to the old gunfire
as they faced their last edged night.

He dies, his name appears instantly
within The Book comes a whirring a click
and ink blossoms on the appropriate page.
The Book then waits.

the callings

     i

mirror/on the wall
       —glass

          an image before

water, rising up:

        echoes
            of light, re-
      bounding, the old faces
    passing solemnly or you, you

        joyfully/with eyes
        open.
           loving me.

ii

a grey hand, smokey
          with laughter
               appears

      & what
it, where it the kin-
ship rises, green waves
        to bow

—ship, gale
are senses within, calm
      ships
        steaming on, twisted
           bright metal speaking
              of the power of waves
                 yet moving inward
                    toward deeper blues

    iii

whirl-
      pools, turning
back time
        to pebbles
shining on the bottom of a lagoon, before
childhood, you, they now return, rightness
belonging to what shines, grows,
moves with sun, with wind
          out of silences.